TOMMY BOMANI
Teen Warrior

Shape-Shifter

BOOK 1

BY: Davy DeGreeff

magic
Wagon

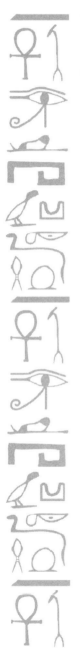

visit us at www.abdopublishing.com

To Ashley, my favorite person in the whole wide world. I couldn't wish for a better muse—DD

Published by Magic Wagon, a division of the ABDO Group, 8000 West 78th Street, Edina, Minnesota 55439. Copyright © 2010 by Abdo Consulting Group, Inc. International copyrights reserved in all countries. All rights reserved. No part of this book may be reproduced in any form without written permission from the publisher.

Calico Chapter Books™ is a trademark and logo of Magic Wagon.

Printed in the United States.

Text by Davy DeGreeff
Cover illustration and chapter art by Sam Brookins
Edited by Stephanie Hedlund and Rochelle Baltzer
Cover and interior design by Jaime Martens

Library of Congress Cataloging-in-Publication Data

DeGreeff, Davy, 1984-
  Tommy Bomani : shape-shifter / by Davy DeGreeff ; illustrated by Sam Brookins.
    p. cm. -- (Tommy Bomani, teen warrior ; bk. 1)
  Summary: After discovering that he has inherited the ability to transform into a cat, sixth-grader Tommy Bomani learns about his Egyptian warrior bloodline.
  ISBN 978-1-60270-697-2
  [1. Supernatural--Fiction. 2. Human-animal relationships--Fiction. 3. Magic--Fiction. 4. Egyptian Americans--Fiction. 5. Youths' writings. 6. Youths' art.] I. Brookins, Sam, 1984- ill. II. Title. III. Title: Shape-shifter.
  PZ7.D36385Tr 2009
  [Fic]--dc22
                                    2009009455

Contents

Dreams

The golden necklace rested heavily around Tommy's neck and filled his body with indescribable strength. He stared at the curved spike, hanging by a fine golden wire from a thick golden chain. It glowed brightly and he was hypnotized by the stone.

Suddenly, the roar of a large crowd snapped him to attention. Tommy jerked his head up and tossed his long, black hair from his eyes. Down a steep, open hill of steps stood the largest crowd he had ever seen. At least 10,000 people were cheering, shouting blessings, and presenting gifts.

Confused but not alarmed, Tommy looked to his left and realized it wasn't only him the masses were so happy to see. Seated in a large throne was a man of great age and overwhelming presence. Atop his head was a simple crown, which contained a stone nearly identical to the one hanging from Tommy's neck. The man's arms were raised, and he smiled affectionately at the people below.

Tommy stood with his arms crossed and his posture straight. He knew the people also cheered for him, their sworn protector. They knew Tommy would sacrifice anything to keep them safe, and they loved him with all of their hearts because of it.

Like an unwelcome visitor, storm clouds began to appear on the horizon, blocking the sun. Rolling thunder overtook the cheering, and the people began to huddle close together. Blasts of lightning suddenly shed menacing light.

The storm quickly grew stronger, blocking all traces of sunlight. Funnels began to swirl slowly, and the people's fear turned into panic. They clambered over one another, searching for safety. Tommy watched calmly, but a great twisting pain had landed in his chest.

The necklace still glowed strongly, but the feeling of safety it lent him dimmed. He knew that this storm could swallow everyone and everything he had worked his whole life to keep safe.

Tommy wasn't afraid he wouldn't be strong enough to fight whatever was darkening the sky. He was afraid he might die, leaving no one to protect his family of thousands.

CHAPTER 1

Reality

Thrown from his seat as the bus hit a bump, Tommy snapped back to reality. The threatening darkness was replaced by the dimness of a school bus well past its prime. Torn seats replaced golden statues and forty bored twelve-year-olds took the place of the crowd of thousands.

Tommy wasn't in Egypt, instead he was on a field trip to the museum. Egypt had been a dream. The same dream, actually, that he'd been having every night for the past two weeks.

Tommy lifted himself out of the aisle and back to his seat near the rear of the bus. No one seemed to notice.

No one except Burt, of course. "You alright?" Burt asked.

"Fine." Tommy glanced over at his friend and tried to give a reassuring smile. He shook a thick strand of black hair from his eye. "Didn't get much sleep."

"Did you have that dream again?"

"Yeah. Except it was quicker. The storm made the people more frightened than the last time," Tommy said, staring at the seat in front of him.

"Sorry, Tom," Burt replied, and Tommy knew he meant it. Burt Miller was his best friend, and the only person he had told about his dream. What he hadn't told Burt was that the dream was becoming more real.

In the beginning, Tommy would watch the people cheer for their pharaoh as if they were on a movie screen. Now he could smell the incense burning and feel the wind whipping by. Each time, the dream felt less like a part of his imagination and more like an uncovered memory.

"Do you wanna talk about it?" Burt asked.

For the first time that morning Tommy smiled. "No, thanks. Maybe later."

The bus lurched to a stop and his smile faded. He turned his attention to the gigantic gray building they had stopped beside. On the building a waving banner declared, "The State History Museum Presents: Archaeology of the Ancient Roman Civilization! Sept. 8-12!"

At the front of the bus, Mrs. Ritchie stood and addressed her class. "Okay, class. Everyone take turns entering the aisle. No pushing, no loud talking, and no jumping down the steps. Wait with your walking buddy until everyone has exited the bus."

Every kid immediately began shouting to their friends and jumping into the aisle. Tommy swung his legs out and started to stand, but was immediately shoved back into his seat.

Though he didn't really need to, Tommy looked up to see who had decided to make his morning just a bit worse. Derrik Jackson smirked and ran a hand through his greasy, dark blond hair.

"Oh, sorry. Didn't see you there, Sideshow," Derrik said, chuckling like he had just said the funniest thing in the world. *Sideshow* and *Circus Freak* were Derrik's clever nicknames for Tommy. Tommy's slightly-smaller-than-average size made him worthy of extra attention in this small-town bully's eyes.

If it wasn't for Burt, Derrik would have been the largest boy in class, so he liked to pretend that Burt didn't exist. Derrik was really good at ignoring facts when they didn't suit him. Of course, the fact that Burt was bigger didn't matter since Burt was anything but a fighter.

"Derrik . . . ," Tommy started, his lips pursing and his hands balling into fists.

"Whoa! Is the Freak gonna say something back today?" Derrik sneered.

Tommy's chest burned, but just as quickly as it came, the flame sizzled out. Tommy resigned himself to letting it go, as usual, and replied, "Never mind."

"Ha! Thought so!" Derrik laughed and butted heads with his partner in crime, Shawn Smart. Then, the two bullies turned and marched to the front of the bus.

After the boys disappeared, Tommy began to move forward, already dreading the day ahead of him.

CHAPTER 2

A Mysterious Man

Even in his sour mood, Tommy couldn't help feeling slightly more relaxed once he stepped through the museum's huge glass doors. He knew he would have no trouble wandering the halls all day. After all, he had done just that many times before.

The State History Museum was incredible, and why it was in Tommy's suburban town he had no idea. His mother had been bringing him there at least every other week every summer for as long as he could remember. It wasn't long before the museum had begun to feel like a second home.

Tommy rubbed his eyes. Something was off. It felt as if something inside the museum was trying to get his attention. Then, he realized he hadn't gotten much sleep the past few nights. It shouldn't be a surprise that he was having trouble focusing.

"Tom! Come on!" Burt waved him toward the patron service desk where the rest of the class had moved. There, Tommy saw the prettiest girl in Mrs. Ritchie's class, Lily Walker. He watched as she ran up and hugged a roundish man who happened to be the museum curator.

Lily was the curator's daughter, and perhaps the only one in their class more familiar with the museum than Tommy. But, her olive skin and green eyes had always been a bit too intimidating for him to walk up and start discussing Chinese artifacts with her.

Tommy followed Burt and quietly thanked Mrs. Ritchie when she handed him a green paper wristband. He didn't feel like traveling with a group today, so he tugged Burt in the opposite direction of their class.

They didn't get more than three steps toward the Egypt exhibit before they saw Derrik and Shawn heading the same way. Tommy quickly changed direction and moved toward the long hall that led to the traveling exhibits.

Egypt would have to wait.

"Rome it is, I guess," Tommy shrugged. Tommy and Burt moved toward a temporary exhibit of ancient Roman artifacts. Ahead of them shuffled a very old man. The boys caught up with him as he struggled with all his strength to open the door.

"Youth before beauty," he croaked. But his drooping eyelids couldn't hide dark eyes that sparkled with youth and strength. Those piercing eyes examined Tommy until he began to feel uncomfortable.

"Thank you, sir," Burt said. He turned slightly sideways to better fit his broad shoulders and edged through the doorway.

"Thanks," Tommy said as he followed Burt, unable to break eye contact with the strange man.

"Enjoy the exhibit," the man said with more than a touch of a foreign accent. He stepped inside the room and let the door close, but moved no farther.

Tommy turned to see where Burt had gone. He found him already studying a diagram of the great Roman aqueducts. Apparently Burt hadn't noticed anything strange about their encounter.

Tommy turned back to the doors. He strained his eyes in every direction, but no trace of the hunchbacked man in the long, dark coat could be found. The man had disappeared.

Tommy and Burt were standing before a marble statue of Roman emperor Marcus Aurelius. Burt's eyes were glued to the list of quotes by the great philosopher-king. He had an abnormal interest in philosophy for a twelve-year-old. It usually cracked Tommy up to hear his friend ponder the details of existence.

Lost in scattered thoughts and with his head throbbing slowly, Tommy followed Burt rather than actually looking at the exhibits. The two boys were edging closer and closer to a heavily secured area full of cameras and red felt ropes.

Soon, they found themselves with their class, who entered through the double doors. A museum guide named Sonji was telling the class about the object that was the reason for all the security.

Working his way to the front to hear better, Burt moved his mountain of a body through the crowd. Tommy followed until they stopped at the first line of ropes. Suddenly Tommy heard a buzzing, like a hundred high-pitched insects were trapped inside his head.

Tommy closed his eyes and listened to Sonji. She explained that this archaeological find indicated that exchanges between Rome and Egypt may have existed hundreds of years before historians previously thought. The buzzing grew thicker and was joined by a low hum. Tommy fought to concentrate.

"What's even stranger," Sonji said, her voice sounding a mile away, "is that this particular object was discovered by itself atop a podium. It was found in what would have been—in ancient times—a highly secure room. The room was hidden in a labyrinth under the Roman senatorial hall. This indicates the piece had immense value. It is speculated that this golden spike may have been a prized possession of the pharaoh of Egypt."

Tommy's eyes snapped open and he stared at the glass case. Inside was the same golden spike that had been in his dreams every night for the past two weeks.

Tommy's head now filled with a dizzying fog. In the second before he fainted, he saw the old man leaning against the far wall observing everything.

Disappearing Act

Tommy slowly awoke and found himself flat on his back. He cracked his eyes open, and the bright light fired a fierce pounding in his head. A fuzzy shape worked its way into view. Piece by piece, Tommy recognized his friend.

"Mrs. Ritchie! He's waking up!" Burt shouted. He turned back to Tommy and asked, "How ya feeling, Tommy?"

Burt hadn't bothered to lower his voice, and it made Tommy wince. Tommy was more than happy to see Mrs. Ritchie nudge Burt aside.

"Yes, Tommy, how are you feeling?" his teacher asked softly.

"I have a headache. Why am I on the ground?" Tommy suddenly realized that he was outside, lying on the grass. Having his best friend and teacher hover over him sent uncomfortable shockwaves through his body. He quickly sat up.

"You fainted," Mrs. Ritchie said, carefully peering into Tommy's eyes. "You didn't appear to be having a seizure, so we brought you out here

15

before calling an ambulance. You've only been outside for a minute. It seems that man was right; all you needed was a little air. Sonji, I think he's okay. Please call his mother and let the staff know."

"Okay. You alright, Tommy?" Sonji asked.

"Yeah, sure."

"Good." Sonji smiled, then turned and hustled back through the doors.

"What man?" Tommy blurted.

"Do you remember the man who opened the door for us?" Burt asked. "He was there when you fell over. He made sure you weren't hurt before most of us even knew you had fainted. I don't know if he was a doctor or what, but he said you'd be fine. He said you just needed a little fresh air. It's a good thing he was there."

"Is he still here? I'd like to, um, thank him." Tommy felt odd about immediately distrusting the stranger. But the way the man had looked at him, vanished, and then reappeared was peculiar. He had a strange sensation that something was off.

"Oh, he was just here . . . ," Mrs. Ritchie said.

"He must have left when he saw Tommy was okay," Burt said.

"Oh. Alright," Tommy sighed.

"Anyway, how is your head now, Tommy?" asked Mrs. Ritchie.

"Um, okay, I guess. I feel a little bit better." Thankfully the buzzing and humming had disappeared, but the numbing headache from earlier had returned. It had already been a very long day, and it wasn't even noon yet.

"Good. Then I guess we can head back in. You don't want to miss lunch," Mrs. Ritchie smiled. A loud growl from Burt's stomach seemed to agree. Mrs. Ritchie turned and started back toward the building, with Burt and Tommy right behind her.

The rest of the day passed by in a blur. Tommy tried forcing himself to enjoy the museum, hoping the familiar surroundings would somehow pull him out of his funk. But after seeing Derrik reenact his fall for a small crowd of entertained classmates, all hope was lost.

Eruption

Tommy and Burt waited a good thirty seconds after the rest of the class got off the bus before they exited. Derrik and Shawn were leaning against a dumpster across the lot waiting for them. Eyeing his prey, Derrik smacked Shawn's arm and pointed.

Tommy sighed and hung his head. His headache had become worse on the ride back to school. It wasn't as bad as it had been right before he passed out, but it was still painful enough to keep him on edge.

Luckily, he had Burt there to do the thinking for him.

"Maybe we should go, um, now," Burt said. He began moving toward home without turning his back on the approaching predators.

"Good idea," Tommy said as he followed Burt. They moved around the bus as quickly as possible without breaking into a run. The last thing they wanted to do was coax Derrik and Shawn into chasing them.

"Maybe they won't do anything today. Maybe they'll leave us alone because of how you're feeling," Burt suggested nervously.

"I wouldn't bet on it."

Burt glanced back without missing a step. He was happy to see their pursuers still hadn't covered the space between them. After all, it was only about a mile's walk to their neighborhood. If things started looking bad before they made it, they could duck in a convenience store halfway there for safety. Derrik and Shawn wouldn't try anything in full view of adults.

Tommy and Burt reached the edge of the store's parking lot and decided to take a shortcut. They hadn't seen their human shadows since the bus, but they weren't naive enough to think the bullies had just given up.

After a few steps onto the parking lot, the dream of a clean getaway faded on the breeze. A thick arm shot out from between two parked vans and grabbed Tommy, yanking him between the vehicles. He twisted out of the grip and stared up into Derrik's ugly face. Shawn grabbed Burt and pushed him next to Tommy.

Rage began to heat Tommy's stomach and work

its way up his body. He could feel the fire coursing through his veins. It fed off the thoughts of his terrible day. One more annoying event was not something he needed.

"Your face looks a little red, Bomani," Shawn sneered.

"Yeah, you aren't gonna pass out again, are ya?" Derrik added, and the two burst into laughter. Derrik shoved Tommy and taunted, "I thought fainting was for girls, Freak. You gonna wear a dress to school tomorrow?"

"Don't touch me," Tommy spat through gritted teeth.

Burt had lowered his head, accepting the inevitable. Normally Tommy would have done the same, but today was not a normal day. It seemed like Fate had chosen this day to bring all its weight down on him. Fate, just like Derrik, had decided to pick on him.

Tommy was sick of being picked on.

"Or what? What're you gonna do, Freak? Faint and hope your head stubs my toe?"

Derrik and Shawn's laughter echoed in Tommy's head, magnifying the dull throbbing. His ability to focus on the simple task of breathing evaporated for the millionth time that day. Frustration was ready to erupt from every part of his body.

Tommy closed his eyes and rubbed his temples, trying desperately to massage the pain away. Instead, it grew. In an explosive release of energy he threw his hands blindly into the air and screamed. He felt one of his fists collide with a smooshy, angry object. A smooshy object that felt exactly like Derrik's ugly face.

Tommy's yelling stopped.

So did the laughter. Well, Derrik's did, at least. Burt's jaw dropped and the color drained from his face in fear. Derrik's face turned a shade of red so dark it could very well have been purple. Realizing he may not get another chance, Tommy leaped between the attackers and sprinted for daylight.

"Sideshow! You're dead!" Derrik roared. The words had no meaning to Tommy. All he could concentrate on was running. He was smaller and faster than Derrik. If he could get enough of a head start, he just might be able to reach his house and see another day.

Tommy found himself praying to anyone who would listen to help him out of this jam. Any fight he had built up had disappeared and been replaced with the simple urge to survive.

Tommy sprinted around the store and down the narrow alley. He readied himself for the final stretch of backyards and swing sets, and nearly smacked into a brand-new wooden fence.

When did that go up? he wondered, frantically trying to figure out how the very worst possible thing could have happened.

He spun in circles, trying to find refuge but found none. He was surrounded by a fence, two walls, and an alley opening that would soon bring the beginning of the end of his life.

Tommy dropped to the ground and waited. He tried to imagine he was someone who wasn't about to be pounded through the cement. A person, an animal, it didn't matter. Just someone who wasn't Tommy *Stinking* Bomani.

Seconds later, two large boys entered the alley, hungry for revenge.

Impossible

Tommy looked up from the ground and did his best to not radiate fear. The sun cast evil shadows across the bullies' faces, leaving Tommy to guess at the devilish scowls they wore. But even without seeing their expressions, Tommy could tell something wasn't quite right.

Derrik and Shawn had stopped walking and were darting their heads around in every direction. They took a couple hesitant steps and continued to glance every which way, like they were expecting something to pop out at them.

"Where did he go?"

"Where did I go? I'm right here, dummy!" Tommy wanted to scream, but wisely kept to himself. He looked at his hands and then his faded red T-shirt, wondering how those two monsters could possibly be so—wait a minute.

Tommy's breath caught in his throat. He blinked once, and then again for good measure. Slowly, he looked at his hands, his eyes growing wider. There weren't hands attached to his arms at all. Instead—

"There's nobody here but a stupid cat," Shawn muttered.

—PAWS! And attached to the paws weren't Tommy's tan, bony arms. Instead, there were gray, finely combed, incredibly furry cat arms! In fact, all of Tommy had turned far more gray and furry than it had been only moments ago.

Derrik stood in a pose that would have represented deep thought in other people and looked at Tommy. Tommy froze, unable to process what had just happened. Surely he hadn't—

"He musta climbed the wall," Derrik said. He took one more good, long look around the alley, then continued, "We'll get him tomorrow. He can't keep walking around with his arms attached after what he did to me." And with that, Derrik and Shawn turned and slowly walked away.

Tommy closed his eyes, refusing to believe what he had just seen. How could he have fur? He was a boy, not an animal. He squeezed his eyes even harder. If he didn't see something, then it wasn't there, simple as that.

But he had seen something, and apparently so had Derrik and Shawn. They had seen something that was impossible.

Tommy figured opening his eyes would be like ripping off a Band-Aid. The faster he did it, the more painless it would be. Preparing himself for the worst, Tommy looked directly down at his silvery gray, fur-covered arms. Only, they weren't fur covered at all.

Not one part of his body even closely resembled an animal. He frantically checked every inch to be sure. He was just average, twelve-year-old Tommy, who had apparently recently begun imagining things. Or had he?

Shawn and Derrik had just been here, he was sure of that. How had they not seen him? And didn't one of them say something about a cat?

Tommy's head began to swirl. That's when he noticed his headache was gone. Every last bit of dull throbbing and crashing pain had evaporated. It was almost as if that had been a part of the dream he must have just woken up from.

Of one thing he was certain: standing in this alley was not going to answer his questions. He needed someplace private where he could think.

Tommy crept to the mouth of the alley and peeked out. When he was sure the coast was clear, he darted past the convenience store and ran as fast as he could.

Tommy didn't stop until he had slipped into his basement bedroom. Panting against the door, he pressed it shut.

CHAPTER 6

Mind's Eye

"I can't tell you right now. Just come over. Burt, this is important. Okay, see you in a couple of minutes." Tommy pushed the off button and tossed the phone on the floor. Then, he lay back on his bed, burying his hands in his hair.

Tommy's mind raced with so many questions that everything blurred into a swirling tornado. At least when Burt got here he'd be able to talk about it. Tommy always thought better when he said things out loud. But how could he describe what had happened without sounding crazy? Maybe calling Burt wasn't such a good idea.

"Tommy?" Tommy's mother called. "Tommy, are you in there? I didn't hear you come home. Why is your door locked?"

Tommy had barely noticed himself locking the door. He had also closed the blinds, changed clothes twice, and put the football cards scattered on his floor into one neat pile. He had done nearly everything he could think of to try to trigger his brain into thinking straight. So far they had all done squat.

"I'm, um, trying on underwear." This was also true. In the past twenty minutes, Tommy had put on and taken off seven pairs of underwear, for no particular reason he could think of.

"Okay. Do you think you could maybe put on some pants and talk to me for a second?"

"I guess." Tommy was in fact already fully dressed, so he paused for a few seconds before opening the door. His mother, a short, beautiful woman with pale white skin and large gray-blue eyes, stood outside the door in her work clothes.

"What's up, Mom-arino?" Tommy grimaced at his attempt to sound casual.

"I just wanted to let you know that I have a meeting tonight," she said. "So I left you pizza money on the counter. Call Burt if you want, once you get your homework done."

"He's-already-coming-over-and-we-don't-have-any-for-tonight-because-we-went-to-the-museum-today." Tommy's words rushed out in one breathless sentence. Tommy had never done well with hiding things.

"Mrs. Ritchie called me, sweetie. How are you feeling?" A look of motherly concern swept over her face, which made Tommy blush. That look always made him feel like such a little kid.

"I'm fine, Mom. I just got a little dizzy."

"Are you sure? Let me know if you start feeling sick again, okay?" Tommy nodded, and his mother pushed a strand of hair out of his face. He could see in her eyes something was on her mind.

"How've you been, Lil' Warrior?" she asked, using her nickname for him. He knew it came from their last name meaning "warrior" in Egyptian. But lately, she only used it when she knew he was upset.

"I'm sorry I haven't been home much the past couple weeks. It feels like you're growing up without me. Every time I come home you look more like a big, strong man. Like your father."

Tommy's stomach dropped. It was always difficult when his mom began talking about his dad, who had died when he was only four.

"Don't worry, Ma. Everything's . . . fine."

"Okay, good." She studied his face, so he forced a smile.

"I'm great." He really hated to lie to his mother, but something just wouldn't let him tell her what was going on. Not until he was sure he wasn't crazy.

She sighed, then glanced at her watch. "Okay, honey. I have to get going, but you and Burt have a good time, alright?"

"Okay, Mom. You too."

"I will." She pecked the top of his head, then turned around and narrowly missed Burt, who rumbled down the stairs.

"Hi, Mrs. Bomani. Bye, Mrs. Bomani," Burt said as he passed by. The boys waited till Tommy's mom cleared the stairs and was out of sight. Then, they shut and locked the door once more.

"Come here!" Burt grabbed Tommy by the shoulders and twisted him around as he checked every inch of him. "You don't have any bruises. How do you not have bruises?" he asked frantically.

"Wha—?"

"If somebody hits Derrik Jackson in the face, they don't live to their next birthday. But you don't even have a mark on you," Burt mumbled.

In the confusing excitement of the past hour, Tommy had forgotten. He had punched the school bully square in the face!

"Oh yeah . . . um . . . that's actually what I called you over about," Tommy stuttered.

"Did you outrun them? Or did you hit him again? Tommy, did you beat up Derrik?" Normally Burt was cool and levelheaded, but when he became excited, it was nearly impossible to slow him back down.

"No, I didn't touch him. Or Shawn. What happened was . . . weird." Tommy bit his lip, struggling for the right words. The explanation he chose had to be perfect. It had to sum up the whole mind-shattering experience, and at the same time, it had to seem believable and logical.

"I turned into a cat," Tommy blurted.

Sometimes simple was good too.

Burt paused. "You what?"

"I turned into a cat." Tommy stared his best friend in the eye and kept a deadly serious face. "After I hit Derrik, I started running, right?"

He told the whole story as Burt listened, his expression changing from fright, to shock, to joy, to doubt. By the end of the story, however, Burt realized that Tommy had never once lied to him. He knew he wasn't lying now. That's when his expression changed to absolute amazement.

"Wow. So . . . you're a boy-cat, then?"

"I don't know. I guess? I mean, it was just that one time. I haven't turned since then."

"Have you tried?" Burt asked.

Tommy paused. He hadn't. He had been so wrapped up trying to figure out if he actually had been a cat in the first place, he hadn't stopped to see if he could change back again.

"No, I guess not."

"Well, maybe you should. Just to see."

"I suppose it couldn't hurt." Tommy moved to the center of the room and looked at Burt, who nodded supportively.

"Good luck," Burt offered.

"Thanks." Tommy closed his eyes. "Burt, I have no idea how to do this."

"That's okay. You'll figure it out. It might take some time though." Tommy smiled, glad he had told Burt what had happened. Even in this crazy situation his friend never doubted him, and it was just the support he needed.

"Maybe you should try thinking like a cat does. Like about fish, and um, litter, and stuff," Burt suggested.

"Think like a cat?"

"Or not, if you don't think it will work."

"No, no, that's a great idea. Worth a try, at least." Tommy squeezed his eyes tighter.

He searched for what to focus on next. He started as Burt had said, imagining himself swatting at fish in a stream with a furry paw, claws outstretched. Then he pictured himself nuzzling a little patch of carpet a sunbeam had warmed. He pictured himself walking nimbly along the top of a fence. Then he was running from a dog, the sound of its panting falling farther behind, and—

"Tommy?"

His concentration snapped and his eyes opened wide. Burt looked over from where he sat on the bed.

"Was it working?" Burt asked.

Tommy thought for a moment. "I don't think so. I think that if that was how it worked, I'd probably be a cat by now."

"Oh, sorry." Burt slouched a little.

"Don't worry, it was a good idea. Besides, I was too afraid to try anything else." Then, an imaginary lightbulb burst into a million tiny shards above his head. Tommy knew he had stumbled on the answer.

"When I turned into a cat, I was scared. I was so scared that Derrik was going to crush me that I just started concentrating on being somebody or something else so I could get away!"

Burt looked skeptical. "Being scared turned you into a cat? Wouldn't it have made more sense for you to turn into a bird, so you could fly away?" he asked.

"Yeah, probably. But then my thoughts changed. I was wishing that I could do more than just hit Derrik and run away. I was wishing that I could fight back for good, and win," Tommy was talking so fast the words nearly blended into one. "I wanted to win like a warrior! This is it, Burt, I know it is. All I've got to do is . . ."

Tommy shut his eyes once more, but they closed gently this time, and his lips rose into a slight smile. Tommy pictured himself as a warrior. He was tall, strong, brave, and wearing a golden chain with a golden spike around his neck.

That was when Tommy heard Burt scream.

CHAPTER 7

Questions

Burt fell from the bed and backed into the corner, his eyes never blinking. He worried that Mrs. Bomani hadn't left yet, so he clamped a hand over his mouth while continuing to scream. He pointed his other arm at Tommy, his finger quivering helplessly in the air.

A gray house cat had suddenly appeared where his best friend had stood only seconds before. When it approached, Burt was unable to move to escape it.

The gorgeous, shimmering gray cat strutted toward Burt. Then, it nuzzled his outstretched hand, purring loudly. Burt stopped screaming. In fact, he nearly stopped breathing.

The cat darted to the other side of the room. There, it crouched and jumped to the top of Tommy's bookshelf, which stood at least six feet high. Not wasting a second, it leaped the five feet to Tommy's dresser without stumbling or sliding. Then, it jumped back toward Burt, landing softly on the bed. For a grand finale, the feline did a backflip, landing out of Burt's view.

Burt was shocked back to life. He scrambled to his knees and shuffled around the edge of the bed. When he got to the other side, he found Tommy lying on his stomach, his chin perched on his fists. A smile covered the lower half of his face.

"How?" Burt dropped to his stomach and stuck his head under the bed. Unsatisfied, he sat back up and began to tear off the pillows, and then the blankets. "How did you do that? Where is it?"

"Where is what?"

"The cat! This has to be a joke!" Burt was so frantic Tommy couldn't help but laugh until his sides ached and it was hard to breathe.

"There is no cat. I told you, I'm the cat."

Burt quit searching and sat down on the bed, shaking his head. His hair now stuck out in unruly bunches, crumpled by his frustrated hands.

"People don't turn into cats."

"Well, I guess I do." Tommy shrugged. "What did it look like when I changed?"

"At first you were there. Then you were all wavy, like I could see through you. Half a second later, there was a cat there. Tommy, where did your clothes go? The cat wasn't wearing them."

"I don't know. Maybe they turn into my fur."

"Aren't you scared? This isn't exactly normal." Burt looked into Tommy's eyes.

"No. Not really." Tommy paused, then started again, "I mean, maybe I was the first time, but not now."

Tommy stood and began to pace the room. "Burt, it felt so natural. Like I'd been a cat my entire life."

Burt's face twisted. "Well, have you? I mean, is this really a new thing, or are you just telling me about it now?"

"Do you really think I could keep something like that from you?" Tommy said in disbelief.

"Maybe we should tell your mom," Burt suggested.

"First, she's left for her meeting by now. Second, no way! I don't want my mom finding out her son is some kind of crazy shape-shifter."

Burt looked seriously at Tommy. "But what if she knows why you can suddenly change into a cat? Wouldn't you want to find that out?"

"If she knew something like this, don't you think she would have said something?"

"Maybe this was just so big, she had no choice. Or maybe someone else wasn't letting her tell you."

Tommy smiled. "I think we're getting away from the point. I'm not going to tell my mom, at least for now, so let's drop it. At this moment, I don't care about why I can change, or how I can change. All I care about is how I can use this to have some fun."

Tommy smiled and stood taller than he had in weeks. Burt looked at him, then took a deep breath and shook his head.

"Well, you sure are in a better mood than I've been used to lately."

"Dude, I feel like I could take on the world. Now why don't we go see what I can do?"

CHAPTER 8

A New Record

The old oak leered over them, blocking the sun. Gnarled branches twisted at menacing angles and black crows cawed angrily from unseen places. Faded chunks of fabric clung to the wood, remnants of failed adventures.

"The Forbidden Oak. No one's ever made it higher than the seventh branch," Burt whispered with fearful awe. "Rob Johnson fell from the fourth branch and broke his arm."

"Angela Follet broke her leg before she even got to the third, and they say she was incredible," Tommy added.

"Are you sure you want to do this?"

"More sure than anything." Tommy stared intently at the tree. "Is anyone looking?"

Burt checked all directions. "I don't think so. Better make it quick. You know, if you can."

Tommy closed his eyes tightly, and within a few short moments, transformed into a sleek cat.

"I hope you know what you're doing," Burt said. Tommy gave a quick nod and sprang up the base of the tree. He made it to the first branch within a couple seconds. Without pausing, he leaped to the second and third branches. He scurried across a large open gap to the next, making it look easy.

By the fifth branch he was taking his time, mentally measuring the distances and routes. From there he leaped to the sixth, and scaled the bark to the seventh. By the time he reached the eighth branch, only a minute had passed since he had left the ground.

Tommy was fairly sure the thick branch would support his human weight. So, he secured a good hold and transformed into his normal appearance.

"I did it!"

"Yeah! Now don't fall!" Burt hollered back. "I don't want to be the one to tell your mom what happened this afternoon."

"You worry too much," Tommy smirked, pleased with his view. Burt looked like a tiny version of his usual self. Tommy took in the golden sun dropping over the horizon, then shouted back down through the leafy branches. "Go get 'em!"

"You sure?"

"It's time for me to be more than just Derrik Jackson's punching bag," Tommy announced.

Burt raced to where the other kids were playing. Tommy watched their kickball bounce along the ground as they turned their attention. Everyone paused, then sprinted to the tree.

"See?" Burt panted, leading the crowd.

"No way! Bomani, how'd you get up there?" Dill Mills asked. "That's gotta be a new record!"

"Nuh-uh," Sam Shepard said. "My big brother climbed to the eleventh branch. I saw him do it."

"He used a ladder, Sam. That doesn't count."

"Does too!"

"No, it doesn't," Dill said, rolling his eyes. "Tommy, what branch are you on?"

"Um, the eighth."

"That's it! That's the record! My cousin's neighbor's older brother got to the seventh branch a million years ago. No one's ever gotten higher." A low murmur rose from the small crowd.

"Bomani, this has gotta be the best day of your life!" Dill yelled. "First you clock Derrik, now this."

Tommy was so surprised he nearly fell off his branch. He steadied himself and called, "How do you know about that?"

"Oh, he's telling everybody. He says that everyone should know, so they won't wonder why he's pounding you into the ground."

"Yeah, well . . . I'd like to see him follow me up here. I can outrun, outclimb, and outpunch him. Maybe he should be afraid of me." As the words tumbled out of his mouth they picked up steam. Tommy almost began to believe them.

"Nah. He'd probably crush you."

"I'm bored. Let's go play kickball. I call first up!" Sam yelled.

As everyone made their way back to their game, Burt asked, "Was that what you were looking for?"

"Yeah, I'm the new record holder!"

"Sure, but you didn't exactly get up there in the most honest way," Burt pointed out.

"They think I did. That's all that matters."

"Whatever you say. Now get down, before someone sees a mysterious gray cat where you were just sitting!"

CHAPTER 9

Gunshots

The short walk back to Tommy's house was surprisingly silent. Burt occasionally tried to start a conversation, but eventually he realized that it was pointless.

When they reached the house, Tommy went inside. It wasn't until they were in the kitchen sitting at the table that he finally spoke.

"I'm getting a soda. Want one?"

"Sure." Tommy returned with a can in each hand. He put one in front of Burt and stared at the table.

Burt tried to keep waiting, but the silence wore him down. Finally, he spat out, "You don't have to be embarrassed!"

"What?"

"About getting stuck in the tree. I mean, this whole crazy thing is new to you. How would you know that cats have trouble climbing down?"

Tommy coughed, spraying soda onto the table. "What are you talking about?"

"Well, you haven't said a word since the park. I know you're embarrassed you had trouble getting down. But I think it's important that you get your feelings out instead of boxing them in. That doctor my mom watches every afternoon says—"

"Dr. Jack? Ha!" Tommy's entire body shook with laughter, and tears began leaking out of the corners of his eyes. "Sorry buddy, but I don't think your mom's favorite TV psychologist has anything to say about my problem."

"I'm just saying, keeping things hidden inside can be unhealthy."

"Okay, here it is: earlier today I found out that I can turn into a cat. And, I have no idea why or how. As I was sitting in that tree, it struck me that I hadn't really considered how weird that is."

"But I thought you said you didn't care."

Tommy shrugged. "I guess I changed my mind. I got so excited that I could do something so cool, I didn't want to think about why something so crazy was happening."

Burt wrinkled his brow in deep concentration. "Then let's try to figure it out. I mean, have you ever heard of anything like this happening to anybody else before?"

"Only in comic books."

Burt's face lit up like a Christmas tree. "There's a start! Have you been doused in toxic sludge or contacted by aliens?"

Tommy laughed and slugged Burt playfully in the arm. "Not that I can remember. Although Derrik's ugly enough to be considered an alien."

Burt didn't laugh. "Really though, is there anything you can think of that's happened lately?"

"Well, I've been having those dreams and getting lots of headaches. But I don't know what those would have to do with turning into a cat."

"Were there any cats in your dream?"

"None that I can think of. Just a lot of people and that storm."

"Anything else?"

Tommy concentrated on the past couple of days, trying to think of anything out of the ordinary that had occurred. He looked out the front window and froze. All at once Tommy's heart paused for just a moment.

"Him!" Tommy yelled. Then, he dove to the ground as a gunshot rang out.

CHAPTER 10

A Change of Pants

Burt screamed, flopping out of his chair and onto Tommy. Both boys lay sprawled on the ground, but Burt's incredible mass blocked all signs that Tommy was even in the room.

"Grrt moff mmm!"

"What?"

Tommy's head struggled for daylight and popped out under Burt's armpit. "I said 'get off me'!"

"Are you insane? Somebody's shooting at the house!"

"No, they aren't! Now get up!"

"Okay, but if you die, it's not my fault." Burt rolled to the side and Tommy wriggled out as quickly as he could. Then he burst for the living room. He smacked into the large foyer window, then kicked the wall. Burt lumbered up behind him.

"He's gone!"

Burt stopped and panted with his hands on his knees, a puzzled expression on his face. "Who is?"

"That weird old guy from the museum. He was stopped in front of my house in his car. When I saw him he tried to drive away, but his car backfired."

"No one was shooting?"

Tommy shook his head. "No. What was he doing here? Maybe he has something to do with all of this."

"What do you mean?"

"Before I saw him, I never did anything crazy like that. He must have, I don't know, put a spell on me or something and that's why I passed out."

"A spell?"

"Yeah. Like a wizard or something. And now he's coming back to check up on me!"

"Should we go after him? Do you think we could catch him?"

Tommy thought for a second. "No, he's gone."

"Then what do we do?"

Tommy ran his hands over his hair in frustration, then he shrugged. "Let's order a pizza. I'm starving. Then we can lock all the doors and windows and shut all the shades. We might even want to grab my dad's old baseball bat from the garage, in case that guy comes back."

"Should we call your mom?"

"If he comes back we will. Besides, we aren't even totally sure what's going on yet. I think that for now we just keep this to ourselves. But we should be extra careful, just in case."

"I don't know, Tommy. A lot of weird stuff has been happening. Don't you think we should tell an adult? Your mom might know how to help."

"For all I know it wasn't the same old man and I'm just seeing things. If anything happens that we can't handle, we'll tell my mom, okay?"

Burt looked at Tommy, obviously unhappy. He crossed his arms. "Okay."

"Good. Let's get started. I'll lock windows and doors up here, and you get the curtains and windows in the basement. When we're done the pizza should be here, and we can eat down in the family room. That's probably the safest place for now."

"Alright," Burt reluctantly agreed.

"Great." Tommy reached as high as he could and clapped Burt on the shoulder. "Let's get it done." Tommy stepped to begin pulling the living room shades, but Burt caught his arm.

"Tommy? Do you maybe have a larger pair of pants somewhere? That might fit me?"

"Yeah, we have some of my dad's clothes still around. Why?"

Burt quickly glanced down at the ground and began rubbing his right arm, like a nervous boy asking a girl to a dance. "Well, when that car backfired it was really loud. I got scared, and I already had to go to the bathroom, so—"

For his friend's sake, Tommy nodded his head and said with a straight face, "Yeah, buddy, I'll find you a new pair. You go get started on the basement."

"Thanks, Tommy."

"You got it." Tommy watched as Burt made his way down the basement stairs, then he turned and smiled.

This day just keeps getting stranger, he thought.

CHAPTER 11

A New Kind of Mischief

The next morning Burt had a dentist appointment, so Tommy walked to school alone. He kept his head lowered and his jacket pulled tight to fight the cold morning winds, wishing he had Burt's massive body to shield him. He decided he didn't mind, since it gave him time to think about the previous night's dream.

It had started the same as it always had. But this time, a massive silver panther had burst from the back of the temple and unleashed a thunderous roar. That was when Tommy woke up.

Tommy stepped from the curb onto the crosswalk in front of his school. *Screeeeeech!* The piercing sound of a car's brakes shattered the morning quiet.

Tommy looked up wide-eyed at the shining silver car grill that had stopped inches away from his chest. A man stuck his head out from the driver's side window and yelled, "Watch where you're going, kid! You trying to get killed?"

Tommy's jaw dropped. He hadn't seen the expensive black car when he checked both ways before crossing. It was the driver who hadn't been paying attention to the crosswalk, and who had obviously been driving too fast.

"It wasn't my . . ."

"Sure, it wasn't your fault. Stupid kid." The man shook his head. "Get out of my way. Now!"

Dumbfounded, Tommy stepped onto the curb closest to his school. He heard the tires behind him squeal, but he didn't turn to watch the car leave.

Up ahead, the school bell rang. Tommy bolted through the front doors and into his classroom, nearly tipping over his desk as he dove into it.

"Thank you for that dramatic entrance, Mr. Bomani," Mrs. Ritchie said with a smirk. Tommy's face turned red, and he slouched a bit lower in his seat. The rest of his classmates stopped talking and faced the front, waiting for the morning's announcements.

Before Mrs. Ritchie began, Lily leaned over and whispered, "I heard about the Forbidden Oak. Very brave, Tommy."

Tommy's face turned even redder and a smile crept from the corner of his mouth. Suddenly he couldn't concentrate. Mrs. Ritchie's words bounced off him like pebbles on pavement.

"Joining our class today is a man of extreme importance in our community. He made a wonderful donation to this school last spring, and today he is here to talk to you about the importance of education. Please give a warm welcome to Mr. Marcellus Fisk."

As if on cue, the classroom door swung open and a man stepped through. His hair was as dark as his coal black eyes, and his skin matched the naturally tanned hue of Tommy's. His unsmiling face and slick hair reminded Tommy of the Roman warrior statues from the museum. Tommy's eyes popped open when he recognized the man who had nearly run him over only minutes earlier.

No one moved. All of the children were seemingly hypnotized by his presence. Behind him stalked two powerfully muscled dogs, each half as tall as Burt. The dogs glanced and sniffed at their surroundings, but seemed to have little interest in the students.

When he reached Mrs. Ritchie, Mr. Fisk's face erupted with a smile from ear to ear. He gave Mrs. Ritchie a hug, then turned to face the class.

Amazing, Tommy thought, *he looks like a completely different person.* With a smile on his face and a more relaxed posture, Mr. Fisk's hypnotizing grip on the students seemed to have disappeared. The kids settled into their desks. The dogs stopped next to Fisk, each of them sitting at one of his heels.

"Good morning, class."

"Good morning, Mr. Fisk," the students answered in unison.

"Mrs. Ritchie was right! You are the best-looking bunch of sixth graders I've ever seen." A few of the girls began blushing. A tiny knot began to form in Tommy's stomach, and he didn't know why. "And you're polite. 'Manners matter', as I'm sure your wonderful teacher has told you." Mrs. Ritchie began to blush like some of the girls.

Mr. Fisk smiled again and Tommy could swear he saw his teeth sparkle. There was definitely something about this guy Tommy didn't like, even on top of their first introduction.

"Thanks for the intro, Mrs. Ritchie. Before I go any further, let me introduce my companions. These are my bodyguards, for lack of a better term. I hope they don't affect anyone's allergies. Now, on to why I'm here. Let me ask you kids a couple questions, and you raise your hands to answer. First, how many of you want to have good jobs when you grow up?"

Everybody's hand went up, except for Derrik and Shawn, who kept theirs down to be funny. No one laughed.

"And how many of you want to have a bunch of money?" Even Shawn couldn't resist that one. "Now, how many of you love school and hope . . ."

The words floated past Tommy. It was a talk they'd all heard a million times before.

Everyone in class knows that you need an education to get a good job. What difference will it make if they hear it from somebody so, so—, Tommy paused. So what?

There was definitely something different about Mr. Fisk, but Tommy couldn't put his finger on it. He was sure he didn't like whatever it was, no matter how much everybody else did. Suddenly, Tommy felt mischievous. Something must be done to shake up Mr. Fisk and show the side Tommy had seen. Tommy raised his hand.

"Yes? Do you have a question?" Mr. Fisk's eyes flashed with dislike at the interruption. It was for just a split second, but long enough for Tommy to notice.

"I'm sorry, Mr. Fisk. I just need to go to the restroom, if you don't mind." Tommy put on his most innocent smile.

"Sure thing, bud. But hurry back, we've got some important things I'm about to go over."

"Of course." Not wasting a second, Tommy scooted out of his chair. He hurried into the hall, making sure to leave the door cracked open behind him. Once he was positive no one was around, he made a mad dash for the bathroom. It may have been Tommy leaving the classroom, but it wouldn't be Tommy coming back. At least, not a Tommy any of his classmates would recognize . . .

"You know, kids, I haven't always been the successful, confident man you see before you," Mr. Fisk continued after Tommy left. "I haven't always had money, a great house, and ownership of the largest investment firm in the state. Do you know where I lived when I was your age? An orphanage.

"My parents died when I was very young. I had no close relatives, so the state took me in. I was put in a terrible orphanage where I was treated like an animal."

Fisk began to pace across the front of the classroom, motioning with his arms. His movements appeared even more dramatic next to his statue-still dogs. "By the time I was thirteen, only slightly older than all of you, I realized that this was no way to live. So, I ran away."

Fisk paused for effect, then continued, "I hitchhiked to the nearest city and spent a year living on the streets. I stole what I needed to survive—," Fisk caught himself, his speech overridden by the low growling of one of his dogs. A curious expression crossed his face, and he turned his attention to the sound. "Silence."

The dog immediately hushed, although still looked unsettled. Fisk turned to renew his story. Just as he uttered the first word, both dogs growled in unison, this time a little louder. They crouched their heads low, bared their teeth, and spiked the hairs on the back of their necks.

"Silence." The dogs did not respond, but instead grew slightly louder. "Silence!" Fisk yelled, growing impatient, and the dogs did as he asked.

The room grew quiet. No one knew how to react. A pin dropping would have sounded like a nuclear explosion, but it wasn't a pin that shattered the silence. Instead, it was the mewing of a cat, which had just walked in the classroom door.

"Mew?"

The dogs took off, barreling down the aisles to the door in back, barking the whole way. Seeming to forget the open hall behind it, the silver cat darted into the classroom. It leaped onto the counter, sending both dogs skidding across the tile as they attempted to reverse directions.

The cat jumped from the counter to the top of a filing cabinet in the corner. Then, it quickly spun around and paused. Its two front paws perched on the edge, waiting for a signal. The dogs charged back the direction they had just come, driven by the sight of their frozen prey. They picked up speed and gave up dodging around legs and desks, barreling through anything in their paths instead.

Dill was plowed to the ground when he attempted to run for the door. Lily stood on her seat, screaming and pulling her pigtails. Two boys held each other in a fierce hug, yelling at the tops of their lungs. Burt sat still, his face as white as if a ghost had just entered the room.

The dogs saw the cat a few feet away. They sprang at him, their intended paths forming a narrowing V. The cat jumped from the filing cabinet, flew over the dogs, and landed on the floor. Then, it strutted out the door, leaving his attackers to crash to the ground.

With the cat gone, the dogs sat motionless. What had seconds ago resembled a hurricane now looked like an incredibly realistic mural of Mrs. Ritchie's sixth grade class.

Mr. Fisk rushed to his dogs and made sure they weren't injured. With some reassuring strokes and soft words, the dogs climbed back to their feet. They stood once again at Fisk's heels, although their eyes gave away their lingering dizziness.

The rest of the class stayed frozen, waiting for someone to break the quiet. When Tommy walked in and cheerily asked, "What happened in here?" Burt finally fainted.

Everyone was so busy looking at Burt sprawled across the desk that no one noticed that the dogs refused to take their eyes off of Tommy.

CHAPTER 12

Eavesdropping

That night, Tommy listened for the click of the door as his mom stepped into the garage. He watched with delight as her car backed out of the driveway and into the road. Then, he walked to the back door and took a deep breath, readying himself for adventure.

A ringing telephone stopped him. He ran across the room and picked it up. The voice on the other end made his heart catch in his throat.

"Hi, Tommy!" It was Lily Walker.

"Tommy? Hello?"

Tommy shook his head, realizing he had stopped breathing. He took in a mouthful of air, creating an awkward gasping sound.

"I'm Lily, how are you, fine?" he spat out, then grimaced. "I mean, I'm fine, how are you, Lily?"

Thankfully, she laughed. "I'm great. Tommy, is your mom around?"

"No, she just left. Do you need her? 'Cause I can get her." Tommy didn't know what was going on. For some reason, his mouth had decided to sabotage him. He took a deep breath and tried again. "Why are you looking for her?"

"I'm selling pies to raise money for the museum."

"Wow. By yourself?"

"Yup. Why? Do you want to help?" Lily asked, her voice hopeful.

"Uh, well, yeah, I would. But I kind of . . . have plans. To do stuff," Tommy stammered.

"Oh, that's too bad. I could have used the company."

Tommy tried to swallow, but his throat had closed to the size of a pea.

"Do you know if Burt's home? Maybe he could help," Lily said.

"Burt? No, his family is going out for dinner tonight."

"Okay. Well, would you tell your mom I called? In case she wants to help support the museum?"

"Sure."

"Thanks, Tommy. See you in school tomorrow."

"Yeah. School." Tommy hung up the phone, then gently banged his head against it. If that wasn't awkward, he didn't know what was.

Tommy turned and bolted out the back door and into his yard. He had already hidden a key under a rock so he could get back in later. He scanned the surrounding houses for onlookers and backed into the tall hedges that lined his house.

Positive no one was looking, he flashed a smile and morphed into a silver cat. From this view, Tommy realized that even as a cat he was smaller than average. But as a cat, he didn't care.

Tommy trotted out from the hedges and jumped up playfully, swiping at a moth. He landed with a soft thud and continued across the yard, making his way to the street.

Where would a cat go for some excitement? he asked himself. Turning east, he walked toward town.

Tommy casually strolled down the middle of the sidewalk, loving how different the city looked from a cat's view. The sun had just begun its late afternoon descent and everything was bathed in an amber glow. People leaving work for the day had begun emptying into the streets, scrambling to their cars and bus stops.

Passersby giggled at the cat smart enough to look both ways before crossing the street. Tommy waited for a young couple to walk right where he wanted. Then he listened to them gasp as he jumped over them entirely and onto a tall fence.

Tommy decided he liked the view even more from up high. He continued along the wooden fence and sat at its corner, which led to an alley. From his perch, he had a perfect view of the people bustling through the streets.

A sleek black sedan slowed to a stop across the street, catching his eye. Out stepped Marcellus Fisk. Tommy's heart skipped a beat. He quickly reminded himself that Fisk would never recognize the cat from earlier in the day. His heart returned to its steady beat.

Fisk opened the back door and led his dogs out by their collars. Instead of walking toward the business center he was parked in front of, he marched the other way. Then, he approached the abandoned building behind Tommy.

Tommy watched Fisk pull open a rusty door and look around suspiciously before entering. Tommy bolted into the alley and looked at the building's windows. A filthy window in the back corner was pushed open and a faint light shone through.

Tommy charged over and poked his head against the mesh screen. He stared into a tiny basement. The walls were bare cement with a single lightbulb. The room was empty except for a few old stools and a large, rickety table near the wall closest to Tommy.

Three men sat on the stools facing the window. The naked bulb cast them in frightening shadows and made them appear incredibly large and threatening. A familiar scent caught Tommy's sensitive nose and he looked in its direction. He recognized Fisk's dogs crouched in the corner.

The table was covered with a hefty sheet of paper, its corners held down by chunks of fallen wall. The seated men didn't glance at the paper but listened to a fourth man. Tommy craned his neck and saw the top of Fisk's head.

"This isn't the time for errors," Fisk said. "Any mistakes made will be dealt with quickly and thoroughly." The men nodded calmly, but Tommy could tell they were scared. "You know who you're doing this for, and you know he accepts nothing less than perfection. Failure won't be tolerated."

With the secret setting, and Fisk's tone, Tommy felt as if he were watching a crime movie. A small burning in his stomach told him to leave, but he stayed put. He thought of an old saying about curiosity killing the cat. Then he shook that off too and concentrated on what was going on below him.

"These are the blueprints to the building. Security checks are here, here, here, and here." Fisk lightly tapped his finger on each spot as he spoke. "The first three we can bypass without trouble. However, if the final security point is fumbled even the slightest bit, alarms go off, gates crash down, and police arrive within minutes. That cannot HAPPEN!"

On the last word, Fisk's fist crashed down like thunder and shook the entire room. Tommy feared the table would splinter in two. The three men shrunk back with shock and the dogs perked their ears, startled by the outburst.

Security checks? Alarms? Police? What are they planning? Tommy wondered.

Fisk worked his way around the table and came up behind the three men. Cloaked in shadow, he gripped the shoulders of the man unlucky enough to be seated in the middle. He lowered his voice to a harsh growl.

"This piece does not belong to this, or any, museum."

The museum? Tommy's eyes widened.

"This piece belongs to those I work for. It has been in the wrong hands for far too long. When our job is completed, we will find ourselves only inches away from fulfilling the prophecy thousands of years in the making."

A prophecy? What do you take from a museum that fulfills a prophecy? Tommy began to mentally run through a list of items at the museum. Nothing came to mind.

"Tonight we show the gods who is king, as destiny has demanded."

Tonight? His head swimming, Tommy stumbled away from the window. He bolted toward Burt's house faster than he had ever moved before.

Alone

"**M**eow. MEOW!**"** Tommy paced outside Burt's bedroom window, meowing at the top of his lungs. He impatiently waited for his friend to notice a cat howling bloody murder.

He glanced quickly around the neighboring yards, then shifted back to human form. The sun had dropped below the horizon, and darkness provided a safe cover.

"Burt! Open up!" he hissed, pounding on the window. Still no response.

Tommy stepped back and looked at the house. Every window was dark.

"Pizza!" he said quietly, remembering Burt's plans for the night. He ran a hand through his hair in frustration. Thankful that his friend's window was open just enough for his fingers to fit, he squeezed them in and lifted up.

Tommy stepped carefully into the basement bedroom. He got chills when he realized that he had just broken into his best friend's house. He shook the feeling off as he searched for the phone.

Tommy had hoped that he and Burt would have been able to figure out a way to stop Fisk. Now that he was on his own, he knew he had no choice but to call the police. After that, he'd interrupt his mother's business dinner so she could bring him to the museum. Of course, that meant he would have to tell his mother what was going on, but he would worry about that when he came to it.

He found the phone on the desk and frantically punched three numbers.

"I'd like to report a robbery. Yes, at the State History Museum." He sat in the desk chair, his head resting on his hand. "No, they aren't there right now, at least I don't think they are. It sounded like they were going to do it later tonight, but it'll probably be pretty soon."

Tommy's brow crinkled with frustration. "No, I told you, they aren't there now. I heard them planning to rob the museum. Does it really matter who's going to do it? Just stop them!" he stopped to listen once again, then closed his eyes and gave a short sigh.

"Marcellus Fisk." He quickly pulled the phone from his ear, surprised by the laughter that came from the other end.

"Look, I'm not kidding, okay? I heard them. They're going to break in, and it's going to be tonight. No, I don't care if you talk to my parents. All I'm asking you to do is send someone by, and just—no, you aren't listening—"

Tommy's eyes widened and his mouth fell open. "He hung up!" He threw the phone at Burt's pillow. "How could they not believe me?"

Tommy's fists curled in frustration and he paced the room. He moved back to the desk and grabbed a pen and some paper.

He jotted down a quick summary of the past hour and put Burt's name at the top. Then, he wiped everything else on the desk to the floor and placed the note where Burt would see it the moment he came in.

Tommy climbed back out the window. If the police weren't going to stop Fisk, then it was up to him. He just hoped he could figure out what he was going to do.

Tommy skidded around the corner, his claws barely keeping him upright. He dashed deep into the alley toward the open window, hoping the thieves were still inside.

The faint light in the window disappeared just as he arrived. He shoved his face to the screen to see the door close, leaving the basement empty. Not taking a second to catch his breath, he dashed back to where he had just come from. This time, Tommy rounded the other corner, tearing a path toward the building's rear entrance.

Tommy once again found himself sprinting across concrete, and he wondered if he had lost his chance to catch them. He rounded a corner and approached another, one that would take him into an alley even more dark and forbidding.

Tommy pulled around the corner so close he felt the ragged brick edges brush his fur. A wall of darkness stood in front of him. He thought to slow down only a half second before he felt his head smash into something as hard as steel. Stars filled his eyes and pain burst through his skull.

All of that was quickly drowned out by a low, familiar growl.

Two growls, in fact. Tommy's eyes adjusted to the darkness and revealed four yellow orbs staring at him. Tommy had found Fisk, but unfortunately, his dogs had found Tommy.

Fisk turned and smiled, cocking his head with bemused recognition. "Well, now don't you look familiar. And judging by these two's reactions, I'd say they recognize you, too."

Fisk's henchmen turned to Tommy, confusion covering their ugly faces.

"Whatchu talkin' about, boss?"

"It seems the . . . cat . . . that created so much trouble for me earlier has found me once again."

The dogs strained against their leashes, snarling and creating pools of slobber on the ground. Tommy felt paralyzed, unable to take his eyes off the fangs so impatiently waiting to sink into his skin.

"What, you mean he followed you? He's just a cat, boss. Cats are too dumb for stuff like that." Something in Fisk's broadening smile snapped Tommy back to reality.

"Most cats, yes, I would have to agree with you. But this cat, I believe, is a little different. Isn't that right, Mr. Bomani?"

Fisk's eyes lit up at the sight of Tommy's small feline jaw dropping.

Then Tommy ran. Fisk's dogs chased after him.

CHAPTER 14

Kidnapped

Tommy could hear the snapping of leashes behind him as they trailed along the ground. He didn't dare look back to see how close the beasts were. He didn't need to look. He could practically feel their hot breath on his neck, waiting to make him into a quick kitty snack.

As Tommy's legs raced, he wondered how long they could keep going. On fresh legs he had made the two dogs look like fools, but now his muscles ached and burned.

Tommy leaped with a quick left into a dark alley. He bolted back out and along the sidewalk as soon as the dogs followed him in. They reacted quickly and stayed on his path.

His legs now had barely any energy. A long night of sprinting had worn them down. He knew he couldn't keep running much longer, and he prayed he had enough energy to transform back into a human. He didn't think it would help him get away, but he hoped that maybe the dogs would be less inclined to attack a person.

Then again, the dogs had his scent, and no amount of shape-shifting could change that.

They were at least two blocks from where the chase had begun and were nearing the end of the building they were running next to. The corner looked to be a million miles away, and Tommy knew he couldn't keep up this pace. The dogs were just too fast, and he was too tired.

Nearing the corner, Tommy took as deep a breath as his exhausted lungs would allow him. Then, he leaped toward the unknown—and into a small duffel bag.

Darkness enveloped him. Through canvas, Tommy heard angry shouts, barking, and the slamming of a car door. He felt himself tossed onto a car seat. He thought about trying to claw his way out of the bag to see who had just kidnapped him. But exhaustion washed over him.

Tommy froze, unsure of what had just happened. He was nervous about the unknown. But he was more relieved that he could no longer smell the sour breath or hear the growls of two large dogs closing in on him.

When the car parked and the engine shuddered to silence, Tommy was instantly alert. Although he was sure he only relaxed for a few minutes, the rest had renewed his energy. Tommy let the reality of the situation kick in. He tensed in preparation for escape at the first chance.

Tommy felt himself lifted in the bag, and he strained to pick up any hints as to where he was. He heard the car door shut, and then a different door open with a loud screech. He heard steps creaking underfoot and the grind of a key inside a lock. Then another door opened.

Finally, Tommy was set onto a solid surface. With a bit of a struggle, the zipper holding him inside was opened. Staying as still as a statue, Tommy waited for something more to happen.

The sides of the open bag still lay over him, blocking his view. He couldn't hear anything moving, but he could definitely smell someone else in the room. Tommy breathed deep, concentrating on the scent. It was familiar, yet unlike anything he had ever smelled before.

"If you wouldn't mind, time is short."

It was the smell of ancient leather tanned by the desert sun. The husky voice rattled Tommy, broke his concentration, and made him catch his breath. He swatted his paws until he found the zippered opening. Then, he pushed it aside and stepped out.

Tommy found himself on top of a small kitchen table in a dark apartment. In front of him sat the weathered old man from the museum. Only now his back was straight and his face in no way gave the impression he was feeble. He still looked old enough to be Tommy's grandfather, but he also looked strong enough to tear a phone book in half.

His eyes rolled along the entire length of Tommy, measuring and assessing, before he spoke. "Please, Thomas, I wish I had more time for formality. But I'm afraid I must ask you to switch back."

What was he talking about? First Fisk and now this? Was there anyone who didn't know?

The man stared straight into Tommy's eyes and put a bit of edge into his tone, "Now, please."

Tommy jumped to the floor, and a few seconds later stood four feet taller. The man's mouth never moved, but his eyes lit up.

"Thank you. Take a seat, please."

Shaking slightly, Tommy's eyes followed the man's outstretched arm. After weighing his options, he moved to sit in a chair across from him. After all, what other choice did he have?

"I suppose you are wondering a great many things," the man began. "Where you are. Who I am. How I know what so few know about you. Unfortunately, we do not have time to answer all your questions. But I hope that answering some will be enough for now." Tommy was surprised to find that he was no longer afraid, and that the man's voice somehow made him feel secure.

"My name, Thomas—"

"Tommy."

Now the man smiled.

"Right, Tommy. My name, Tommy, is Asim. I was a friend of your father's, quite a good friend, actually. And I believe, that he would have wanted me to tell you a story. Or at least the important parts, for this is a tale that would take days to fully tell. So if you don't mind . . . "

Tommy shrugged. "Sure."

The old man shifted in his seat. When he began, his voice was alive, filling the room.

"This story comes from Egypt, the same place your father and I come from. But it begins thousands of years earlier, in the heart of the pharaoh's kingdom. It isn't a story many know, because others have worked to keep it so. It starts with a curious young woman by the name of Bastet, and her equally curious child, Bomani.

"One day, Bastet and Bomani appeared as if from nowhere, amidst a ferocious sandstorm. They were given food and shelter, and were soon made a part of the community.

"As Bomani grew, it became apparent he was not a normal child. It became more and more difficult to ignore that he was special. He was said to never cry, and he was never ill. He also found he had the strange habit of transforming into a cat whenever he pleased.

"Bomani was frighteningly smart and undeniably brave. He quickly grew into a tall, powerful young man. By his eighteenth birthday, he found himself employed as the personal guard to the pharaoh, a position of great importance.

"This pharaoh was much loved by his people. Only one person in all of Egypt held a grudge against him. That person was his younger brother, Badru.

"Badru felt that he was the rightful ruler, and he constantly plotted ways to steal the throne for himself. The pharaoh had heard rumors of Bastet's child, and he was delighted to have such a special man on guard.

"A few years after Bomani was named head guard, a great festival was held. On the final day, the pharaoh revealed to his people a gift given to them. Ra, the king of the heavens, had made them a small, gold statue in the shape of a swirling sun. He had personally delivered it to the pharaoh.

"This statue, Ra had said, would give whomever possessed it great power and extended life. The statue's possessor would rule Egypt forever.

"All the people, save one, celebrated the gift. They rejoiced that they should be allowed to have their pharaoh for all time. The pharaoh's brother, however, was not pleased. He'd had enough of being shoved to the shadows by his perfect brother.

"Badru realized that if he stole the statue, no one would be able to stop him from having what he believed was rightfully his." A scowl now sat on Asim's face, as if a bad taste had developed in his mouth.

"Badru waited until late at night after the festival was over. Then, he tried to steal the statue from its shrine.

"He did not succeed. Bomani realized how powerful a bait the statue would be. So, he laid a trap and watched his prey walk directly into it. Badru was taken to the city gates, where he was pushed out into desert exile."

A Dark Alliance

Asim slowly stood and walked to the kitchen. He grabbed two tall glasses from a cupboard and filled them with water. He placed one in front of Tommy without a word. He took a sip of his water, and when he began to speak again his voice was quieter. He spoke as if telling a story he never wished to tell.

"With Badru banished from the city, everyone —even Bomani—believed that the threat to the pharaoh was gone. But Badru thought differently. The palace guards had forced him outside of the walls and locked the gate behind him. Badru did what only a crazy man would do: he marched straight out into the scorching desert.

"The guards watching reported it to the pharaoh. Though he was sad for the death of his brother, the pharaoh knew it was best for his kingdom. Badru, however, did not die. He lived like a desert hermit and dedicated himself to an evil, ugly magic.

"The time Badru was gone passed peacefully in the city. Every day, the pharaoh and Bomani grew closer. Eventually, it came time for the celebration of Ra's gift. There was food and games, and the city rejoiced.

"By nightfall everyone was exhausted, and they began to quietly retire to their homes. No one noticed the shadow of a banished man sneaking from building to building, making his way closer to the palace.

"Badru arrived at the shrine room after murdering every guard he passed. The beauty and importance of the statue nearly stopped him in his tracks. But he continued, his smile growing larger with every step. Badru raised his hands to either side of the statue but froze when someone called his name.

"'Badru,' Bomani said with calm authority, 'I declare you under arrest by the name of the Pharaoh.'

"Badru turned slowly, and the confident, evil smirk on his face unsettled Bomani. The banished brother looked completely different than he had a year earlier. His fat had turned to muscle, his head was completely shaved, and scars decorated his once pampered face. His shoulders had broadened, and his prowling stance signaled danger.

"Without a word, Bomani knew that Badru had no intention of being captured. Bomani quickly shifted forms. Now, instead of a man there was a silver jungle cat the size of a small horse.

"Bomani expected Badru to quake and to fall to his knees with fear. He didn't. Instead, he laughed like thunder crashing from the heavens. He laughed until all breath had left him. Then, lowering his eyes with scorn at Bomani, he too began to change.

"In an instant, Badru had transformed into a powerfully muscled dog. Its coat was dark as midnight. Bomani was surprised but never frightened. He pounced.

"The two fought with every ounce of their souls. Claws flashed and teeth tore flesh. For what seemed like ages they tangled. Then, with the quick swipe of a large paw, Bomani pinned Badru's throat to the ground.

"Disgusted, Badru batted the claws from his neck and darted deeper into the room. There, he changed back into his human form. He grabbed his cloak from the ground and wrapped it around his shoulders.

"Bomani stayed in his cat form and slowly edged toward the intruder. Badru let Bomani push him back until he was nearly pressed to the statue. Then, an evil look replaced the fear in Badru's eyes, and Bomani stopped. Only then did he realize that he had placed the enemy right next to Ra's gift.

"With lightning speed, Badru spun around, grabbed the statue, and turned back to Bomani. Badru curled his mouth into a disgusting smile, then reached above his head.

"He smashed the statue to the ground, releasing an explosion that was heard for miles. The statue shattered into seven identical, daggerlike pieces, which skidded across the floor and apart from each other.

"Anger and duty coursing through his veins, Bomani leaped toward Badru. But the pharaoh's brother had one more trick up his sleeve. Muttering an ancient word, Badru threw a ball of dark fire directly into Bomani's chest. But even that wasn't enough to stop him.

"Singed and burning, Bomani managed to take one last swipe across his enemy's left eye before he hit the ground. Screaming with outrage, Badru backed up, then tripped on his cloak and slammed to the floor. Realizing that some power may still reside in the pieces, he quickly scooped up two of the golden shards. He staggered to his feet and ran for the exit, limping and broken.

"Bomani cursed himself for failing his friend and master, the pharaoh. Then, he passed into exhaustion."

Tommy sat in complete silence, breathing heavily. When he couldn't stand it any longer, he said, "Did he die?"

"Badru or Bomani?"

"Either one. Did either of them die?"

"Unfortunately for us, no, Badru did not die. He escaped to the desert once more and has only been seen by travelers as the sun begins to set. And fortunately for you, no, Bomani did not die either. Although it was close. Badru was full of incredibly dark magic. Bomani slept for many days before his eyes opened again.

"When he did wake up, he found that quite a bit had happened. The wise pharaoh had discovered that the five remaining pieces of the statue did indeed still hold some power. He also realized that although Ra's intentions had been good, no human man held the wisdom of a god.

"He sent three of the pieces far from each other, with each piece arriving in a location only known to the pharaoh. One of the pieces he had fashioned into his crown. He wore it until the day he died, many years later. The final piece he reserved for his best friend and greatest confidant."

"Bomani?"

"Exactly. He knew that Bomani had done a great service to his pharaoh. He hoped that his piece would be able to help Bomani's descendants retain his amazing powers. And do you know what Bomani did with this piece, Tommy?"

Tommy knew in an instant. "He made it into a necklace."

Asim smiled. "And that necklace has been passed down to the first-born child of every Bomani family ever since. With the exception of one."

CHAPTER 16

Inheritance

Asim turned and looked at Tommy with a piercing gaze. Tommy had no choice but to look back into the old man's eyes.

"As I'm sure you've begun to realize, I've been watching you for some time now, Tommy. What I've seen has not made me exceptionally comfortable. The Bomani bloodline is one of warriors. But you sit before me undersized, a below-average student, and a leader of no one. You are the last remaining descendant of an Egyptian legend, yet you weren't even able to escape me.

"But there is hope. Your father was the same size at your age. Well, maybe when he was a bit younger, but still, he took some time to develop. And while you may not possess the leadership of Bomanis, you have courage. Courage is the lake from which all leadership must flow."

Asim winked. "Certainly a boy without courage would not have been able to fight two large bullies, even if he did eventually run away."

Tommy swallowed, unsure how to feel.

"Then, there is the fact that you—without training or even knowledge of your abilities—transformed without any mistakes. This is nothing short of astounding. Even your father took weeks of preparation before he made a successful transformation. Though, he was two years younger than you are now.

"Keep in mind that I do not make these comparisons lightly. Your father was one of the greatest warriors the world has ever known."

Suddenly Tommy was overwhelmingly proud, both of himself and of the father he barely remembered. Without knowing why, Tommy felt his throat tighten and tears creep to the corners of his eyes.

Asim looked away from Tommy and glanced to the far wall with a clenched jaw. Spotting the clock, Asim's eyes opened wide and he spoke again, this time at a more clipped pace.

"I'm afraid I've lost track of time, and I hope to the heavens that doesn't put us in a worse spot than we already are. Tommy, those men that were chasing you, do you know what they were doing?"

"They were planning on breaking into the museum. But I don't know why."

"Don't you? Think Tommy. Think about what I just told you. Think about where I was when we met at the museum."

Tommy racked his brain. He needed to think only for an instant before the pieces slid neatly into place.

"One of the pieces is there. That's what made me pass out!"

"Precisely. This is no ordinary burglary. One of the pharaoh's selected locations must have been ancient Rome. This piece was uncovered by archaeologists, and it was only a matter of time before Badru learned about it."

A lightbulb flashed in Tommy's head. He guessed, "Are you saying that Badru . . . is Fisk?"

"No. Mr. Fisk is his henchman, a man dedicated to do the ancient wizard's bidding. Badru wouldn't trust a fool with a job this important. Fisk is likely dangerous. Still, you mustn't be afraid when you confront him."

"Me? Why don't we call the police? You're an adult. They'll listen to you."

"No. This is your fight, thousands of years in the making. With every piece he gains, Badru grows stronger and more capable of greater evils.

He must be stopped, and you are the only one who can do it. Badru must know that the Bomani bloodline is resurrected, and that it is willing to stop him at any price."

Tommy sputtered, fear and nerves shaking his lips like dry fall leaves. "What if they have weapons? Knives? Guns?"

"It won't matter. You'll have this." Asim pulled up a small oak box. Its presence instantly made Tommy's head swim. "I believe you have some idea what is inside." Twisting the ancient latch on the front rim, Asim turned the box to Tommy and pulled back the lid.

There it was. Just like in his dreams. The gold dagger practically floated above the cloth lining. It had perfectly straight edges where the break must have happened. One end tapered into a razor-sharp edge, the other wavering in the perfect mimic of a ray of sunshine.

It looked as strong as steel, and as shiny and gorgeous as the day Ra had carved it. Just as in his dream, the top end was attached by a bed of immovable wrapped wire to a thin but sturdy chain. Tommy grasped the chain and pulled the statue from its container with awe. He studied it like a friend he hadn't seen in years.

Tommy curled the chain in his hands and pulled the open loop over his head. When he let go, the statue dangled from the middle of his chest to the top of his waist. It felt as natural and comfortable as anything he had ever touched. The heavy gold necklace filled Tommy's body with strength.

"And now you must go."

Tommy lifted his head, then nodded.

"As an old man I would be nothing but a bother to you. It has always been my role to teach and to guide. After tonight, I will do plenty of that. For now, everything rests on your shoulders."

Tommy reached out and shook Asim's hand. Then, he turned and left the building as quickly as he could.

Trial by Fire

A faint hum floated around Tommy, coming from the dim fluorescent lightbulbs overhead. They were only half lit, providing just enough light to see what was in front of him.

Tommy moved swiftly from the loading dock down the tight corridor that led to the main halls. He wasn't familiar with this part of the museum. But he took comfort knowing that he would soon be walking on tiles he had stepped over a thousand times before.

I know this building too well, he told himself, *there's no way they'd be able to—*

He tripped, barely stopping himself from screaming. Squinting, Tommy fought to see what had driven him to the ground. He immediately wished he hadn't been so curious.

Sprawled against a wall with only the tips of his boots catching weak beams of light sat Rudy, the night watchman. Tommy rushed to his side. Remembering bits of a first aid session from gym class earlier in the year, he put two fingers on the man's throat. Tommy let out a whoosh of breath when he felt a pulse. It was weak, but definitely present. Mouthing a silent promise to return, he moved down the hallway.

Tommy paused in a doorway and stared at the small white box on the wall. Even during the open hours, the museum's security system indicator lights glowed and blinked in this box. Now, they were all dark. Fisk had gotten by Rudy and bypassed the security system. Nothing was giving him trouble. Tommy took a gulp and moved forward, intending to change that.

A voice made him catch his breath, but he started breathing again when he realized it came from the next room. Taking care to move quietly, Tommy edged along the dark walls and hid behind display cases. Slowly, he made his way toward the voice, which had now been joined by another.

The voices were low and quick. Tommy snuck to the doorway and peeked into the next room. There, he saw what looked like a drawing from a comic book brought to life.

Clothed entirely in black, from their ski masks to their combat boots, stood two of Fisk's men. They were staring intently at a piece of Ra's statue.

Between them and the protective glass case was Fisk, who was fiddling with a small silver box. A few feet away from him lay his dogs, their heads moving slowly back and forth, scanning the room.

Does he go anywhere without those stupid dogs? Tommy wondered.

It dawned on Tommy that Fisk must be working on bypassing the final security point, the alarms that would alert police if anything went wrong. He looked at the ground, searching for something to throw to set off the alarm system. Then he stopped and silently yelled at himself. Asim had told him that this was *his* fight.

Taking a deep breath and squeezing his fists, Tommy prepared himself. Then, he began walking toward his destiny. Halfway through his first step, he changed his mind and toppled off-balance against the doorway.

What are you doing?! his brain hollered at him. *Do you even have a plan? Or were you just going to walk up and politely ask them to please leave the building?*

He instantly felt like an idiot. How did he plan to stop three grown men and two gigantic dogs? By turning into a house cat? What good would that do him?

Whatever his plan was going to be, he needed to think of it quickly. The large dogs were no longer scanning the room. They were staring directly at him. And they did not look happy.

Tommy froze. The growls turned to ferocious barks and the dogs charged. Calling upon an instinct he didn't even know he had, Tommy shifted into a cat without trying. He ran directly at them.

Surprised, the three men stood and watched as a sleek gray cat shot out of a side room straight at the monstrous dogs. Suddenly, it changed direction and sent the dogs sprawling across the smooth floor.

They watched, motionless, as the animals zigzagged around the room, skidding within inches of priceless artifacts. Fisk screamed at his men to catch the cat so they could continue their work.

"No annoying child is going to stop us tonight. Grab that cat and kill it!" he roared.

But try as they might, the masked morons could do no more than get in the dogs' way. They even served as an obstacle for Tommy to place between himself and his hunters. Tommy dove between the men's legs and jumped onto their turned backs, tricking the dogs into massive collisions.

Tired by the day's activities, Tommy soon began to slow. The men and the dogs worked together, finally cornering him high atop a sturdy glass case.

Beckoned by Fisk, who had now joined the group, one of the masked men closed in on the feline. With a hiss and a quick charge, Tommy put four bloody scratch marks on the man's hand.

The would-be captor screamed and backed away. The frightening half-circle continued to close in. With a smile, Fisk told them to stop. He yelled toward the room's main entrance.

"Jameson! Bring him here! Now!"

Before Tommy's startled eyes, a third masked henchman pushed Burt into the room.

"I'm sorry, Tom. I got your note and—"

"Quiet!" Fisk screamed. "Are you happy now, Bomani? Instead of simply letting the prophecy play out, both you and your friend now have to die. This is the price of your heroics, my young warrior."

Fisk stepped back and roughly grabbed Burt by the front of his shirt. Then, he threw Burt to the ground in front of the other two cronies.

"Take out your knife," Fisk barked. "If either of them tries to get away, the fat one dies. We may not be able to catch Bomani, but I know he won't leave without his idiot friend."

The man closest to Burt gladly unsheathed a long knife from somewhere along his waist. He playfully swiped it in front of Burt's face. Burt cowered back against the ground.

Fisk pointed and stared directly into Tommy's eyes, which glistened from the shadows. "Don't do anything stupid. I'll deal with you when the statue is mine." He walked back to the glass case and continued to push buttons on his electronic device.

Tommy pushed himself as far back into his dark corner as possible. He turned back into his normal form, not even caring if the glass case underneath him could support his weight.

Then something inside of him changed. Tears began to peek from his eyes from anger, not fear. He had been pushed around as long as he could remember. Until a few days ago, he had never been able to do anything about it. Now these men were threatening to kill him and his friend and attempting to take something that belonged to him more than to anyone else.

Tommy looked down at Burt, covered in his own tears and dodging the taunting knife swipes of three apelike criminals. This was too much.

Tommy's blood began to boil. A growl began deep within his stomach and worked its way to the edge of his throat. Dropping as far into the shadows as possible, he transformed into a cat once again. He stepped confidently to the end of the display case, each step feeling slightly more powerful than the last.

Burt was the first to notice. His eyes stayed on Tommy as if magnetized. He no longer acknowledged the bluffing swipes of the dangerous blade. His mouth dropped open, and he gave a low moan of astonishment.

CHAPTER 18

Victory or Death

"**T**ommy . . ."

The three masked men followed Burt's gaze, and then mimicked his response.

"Uh, boss . . . ," one managed to eek out. He was soon cut off as Tommy unleashed a roar that shook the room's walls.

Tommy was full of anger and fear and a thousand other emotions he couldn't quite place. But he grabbed his courage and leaped at the nearest criminal. Tommy knocked him to the ground and pinned his chest with alarming ease.

Surprised by the fear in the man's eyes, Tommy paused to look at himself.

"Tommy, you're . . . you're huge!" Burt blurted.

He was. Instead of an average house cat, Tommy now appeared as a powerful jungle cat, twice the size of a large dog. His paws, once so small and fluffy, now held down the henchman's chest with claws inches long and as sharp as razors.

His coat was still brilliant silver, but it now covered a sleek, muscle-lined body. On Tommy's chest was a slightly darker patch of hair, the perfect shape of Ra's statue.

Tommy couldn't blame the man for being afraid. He raised his right paw to his left cheekbone. Then, Tommy smashed the back of his paw into the man's face, knocking him unconscious.

The other two cowering crooks stepped back, their eyes wide and jaws dropped. Fisk's loyal hounds soon replaced them. The dogs kept a wide angular wedge, slowly closing the gap between them and their enemy.

Tommy made up his mind and quickly dashed at the dog on the left, throwing him back on his heels. The dog on the right attempted to come to the other's aid, but was too late.

Without a second of hesitation, Tommy reversed direction and swiped the other across its nose. It turned around and bolted straight for the door, never looking back.

Least surprised of everyone in the room was Fisk, who hesitated only for a moment. He marched in Tommy's direction, appearing far more annoyed than frightened.

Tommy wasn't frightened either. In fact, he had never felt better. With every move he could feel muscles rippling with power. When one of the men stepped forward to try his luck, Tommy just smiled to himself.

The man crouched low to the ground, swiping his knife in large arcs at the big cat before him. Tommy paused, then took a tiny step away, the hair bristling on his neck as if afraid. The man took a couple shuffling steps closer, his swipes becoming more confident.

The gigantic cat was now nearly backed against the wall, quivering with fear, just as the knifeman intended. Satisfied with his position, the man switched from shuffling steps to quick, bursting strides. He held his knife chest-high and ready to attack, just as Tommy was hoping he would.

Tommy took a half-step to the right, narrowly avoiding the flashing steel as it slashed through the air. He jumped back to the left as though he'd never been anywhere else. He tackled the man, knocking his blade across the ground and out of reach.

Tommy was ready to unleash all the anger, fear, anxiety, and stress that had balled up in him over the past two hours. He placed his jagged teeth barely an inch from the man's face and let loose a ferocious jungle scream.

The man's eyes watered and his hair flew back like he was on the downslope of a roller coaster. Unable to contain his fear any longer, the man gave one last sob, then fainted.

Tommy turned back to Fisk and his remaining henchman. Without a word the other man turned and ran out the far exit. He nearly knocked Fisk over in the process.

Tommy continued to purr as he inched closer to Fisk. Three down, one to go. Just like his father before him, Tommy had done his duty to protect the Sun of Ra. For once in his life he had done something right, something that he could be proud of. One more man to stop, and no one could say he wasn't a hero.

Then Fisk pulled out his gun and aimed it at Burt.

CHAPTER 19

Confrontation

"I wouldn't recommend coming any closer, Mr. Bomani. For all I know, these bullets would bounce right off your cursed body. I can guarantee your friend would not be so lucky."

Tommy stopped immediately. Burt closed his eyes and bit his bottom lip. He, too, thought they had won. How very wrong they had been.

"I must say, I am impressed. The way you handled those dogs . . . perhaps the prophecies aren't so far off. It's too bad we'll never find out."

Tommy looked on helplessly. He now stood too far away to attack without putting Burt in harm's way. Hoping he was wrong, Tommy silently pushed one paw forward.

"No, no, no, Mr. Bomani," Fisk said as he cocked the hammer on his pistol. "There will be no more of your heroics tonight." Tommy drew back his paw. "In fact, why don't you change back to a more . . . controllable form, just to be sure."

Tommy hesitated, not willing to give up the only advantage he held.

"Unless you would like me to shoot your friend, I strongly suggest you do as I say. I don't have time for annoying bravery."

Tommy took one last look at his powerful paws, then turned back into his normal shape. His piece of the statue hung once again from his neck, heavy as a boulder.

Fisk began to laugh.

"Look at you! Just a boy. And yet you thought you were strong enough to take on the powers of Badru. Powerful as your blood may be, there is no match for the dark powers of true Egyptian royalty."

"Royalty? Badru was just a stupid prince that nobody cared about. His brother was the real pharaoh!" Tommy shouted.

For an instant, a dark cloud passed over Fisk's face, but just as quickly his smile returned. "Defiant until the end. It's that same type of talk that got your father killed. You Bomanis are an incredible breed. It's almost too bad the bloodline has to stop with you."

Tommy threw his arms in front of his face in feeble defense as the gun turned in his direction.

"Badru will be so pleased."

Fisk once again smiled, then began to pull the trigger.

Suddenly a new voice filled the room, "Stop! Police! Put down your weapon!"

Fisk's head whipped toward the entrance and his jaw dropped. Standing in every possible entrance were police officers, all pointing guns at Fisk and moving in closer.

"Put down your weapon and step away from the children!"

Fisk closed his eyes and began to move his head violently, as if having a wordless argument with himself. His arm lowered halfway to the ground and he looked at Tommy.

"Badru may not get the stone this time, but at least he'll get you!" Without warning, his arm raised level once more and pulled the trigger with a deafening bang. Tommy fell to his back and covered his face.

Amazingly, he felt nothing. No holes, cuts, or pain of any sort. With extreme confusion Tommy pulled his hands from his eyes, then let out a shout of joy. Bawling with sheer fright and exhaustion, Burt was lying on top of Fisk and pinning his arms to the ground.

The police officers moved in and pulled the two apart, then placed Fisk in handcuffs. Powerless, on his knees, and with his dark hair now falling anywhere it pleased, Fisk looked far more crazy than intimidating.

"Bomani! You might as well quit now! You got lucky this time, but the rise of Badru is inevitable! I'll be back, and you'll regret your cursed inheritance!"

The officers grabbed Fisk and pulled him to his feet, but not before he could bite one on the hand. Using more force, they pulled him out of the room and out of the museum. A couple of officers stayed behind to begin studying the scene, obviously baffled by the unconscious men. One policeman walked over to Burt, who was now standing with Tommy.

"What happened here, boys?"

His adrenaline gone and shyness returned, Burt looked at the ground. Tommy spoke up, "Just the end of a very long week, Officer."

CHAPTER 20

Just the Beginning

Tommy and Burt now stood together in front of the museum. They were wrapped in warm blankets the police had given them after they were briefly questioned. Both claimed to have been so scared that they didn't remember anything other than wandering into the museum when they saw an open door. Also, neither of them had any idea what one of the men arrested meant when he muttered about a "magical jungle cat."

"How do you think the police knew, Burt? They wouldn't listen to me." Before Burt could speak, the answer to Tommy's question came running out of an expensive sedan that had just pulled up in the parking lot.

"Oh my gosh! Are you two okay?" Lily Walker charged toward them in a full run, then looked them over like a worried mother. Burt's face went so red Tommy thought his head would explode.

"We're fine," Tommy replied with a chuckle.

He did his best to guide her over to Burt, hoping she wouldn't notice the swell of the necklace under his shirt. "Calm down, Lily. You're going to give yourself a stroke."

"Burt, I'm so glad you called me. I can't imagine what would have happened if you hadn't. Just think of all they would have taken if you hadn't made me tell my father!"

Tommy nearly fell over. Before he could even ask the question, Burt interrupted him, "I got your note right when I got home. I figured the police wouldn't listen to me either, so I called somebody I knew they would have to listen to."

Tommy smiled and beamed with pride. Everyone knew that Lily could talk her father into anything. If the museum curator was calling the police, they'd have no choice but to listen.

"Awesome job."

"Thanks, Tom."

Another car had pulled up behind Lily's father's. This one was older and rustier and screeched to a halt. Out stepped Asim and Tommy's mom.

"You guys stay here. And thanks, both of you." Tommy ran between Burt and Lily and made for his mother.

"Mom . . . Asim!" Tommy's mom met him halfway, moving more quickly than he had ever seen her. She grabbed him for a strong hug. Then she put Tommy through his second thorough inch-by-inch examination of the week.

"Oh, you're okay. Thank the heavens," she sighed.

"Mom, I'm fine. Actually, I'm great. Asim, what are you doing with my mom?!" The old man strolled up, taking in all that was going on under the flashing red and blue of the police lights.

"Asim, I did it! I—" Tommy stopped, checking to make sure no one around them could hear. "The stone is safe."

"So it seems. You did well, Tommy."

"That may be true, but he shouldn't have been put in this situation in the first place." Tommy's mom sent Asim a glare Tommy was all too familiar with.

"This may have been a bit earlier than we would have hoped for, but the strength of Tommy's blood and of his character showed through. Just as I knew they would. Your mother is none too pleased with me at the moment, Tommy," Asim said calmly.

"We can, and will, talk about this later, Asim. For now I'm just glad my boy is safe."

"Wait," Tommy said. "She knows?"

"Young man, I'm afraid she knows much more than you might care to believe."

"I'm sorry I haven't been home, Tom. Asim felt you needed the time alone to speed your development. I hated leaving you, but I guess he was right."

Asim snorted. "What I believed was hardly a guess, my dear. I acted upon what I knew was the solution. But these are all things we can discuss later. Tell me, Tommy, did you fight well?"

"You wouldn't believe it. I turned into a full-sized cat. Like, a panther or something. It was amazing."

Even in the dark Tommy could see Asim's eyes light up. "Excellent, excellent. Perhaps you aren't as behind schedule as it would seem."

"What's going to happen to the stone? Is it going to stay in the museum? What if someone tries to take it again?" Tommy's questions rushed out.

"The museum curator is a friend of ours. The stone has been taken off display and is already on its way to a safer place. It will be held until it is needed."

"Needed? What does that mean? And Fisk said something about me fulfilling a prophecy, right after he pulled out his gun. What was he talking about?"

Tommy's mom gasped at the word *gun*, but Asim ignored her and put up his hands in defense.

"So many questions, Tommy, and all good ones. But they are questions for another time."

Suddenly Tommy felt the adrenaline rush he had worked up drain from him. "You mean I just found out that I'm part of some sort of prophecy and you're going to make me wait? I thought you'd told me everything."

"Young man, there are many things I have yet to tell. We haven't even begun to discuss your mother's side of the family."

Tommy's head whipped in his mother's direction. She mischievously shrugged her shoulders. Asim's eyes sparkled.

"When are you going to tell me everything I don't know?"

"All in good time, Tommy," Asim assured him. "Besides, history is part of your training, which is something we're already behind on. For now, let yourself be satisfied with a night of great victory. There are sure to be many more battles, and not all of them are certain to end as well as this one. Go get your friends, Bomani."

Figuring it did no more good to argue, Tommy nodded and made his way toward Burt and Lily.

Prophecies, gods, guns, criminals, and magic, he thought. *I can't wait to see what's gonna happen next week.*

CONTINUE THE ADVENTURE WITH

Tommy Bomani: Teen Warrior

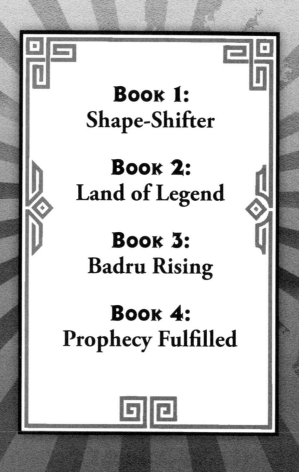